Club Earth

Susan McDonough-Wachtman

Ukiyoto Publishing

All global publishing rights are held by

Ukiyoto Publishing

Published in 2023

Content Copyright © Susan McDonough-Wachtman
ISBN 9789360163181

*All rights reserved.
No part of this publication may be reproduced,
transmitted, or stored in a retrieval system, in any
form by any means, electronic, mechanical,
photocopying, recording or otherwise, without the
prior permission of the publisher.*

The moral rights of the authors have been asserted.

*This is a work of fiction. Names, characters,
businesses, places, events, locales, and incidents are
either the products of the author's imagination or
used in a fictitious manner. Any resemblance to
actual persons, living or dead, or actual events is
purely coincidental.
This book is sold subject to the condition that it shall
not by way of trade or otherwise, be lent, resold,
hired out or otherwise circulated, without the
publisher's prior consent, in any form of binding or
cover other than that in which it is published.*

For Lisa

"Calm down, Mom, okay?" I tried to soothe the agitated voice hissing in my ear. "I'll hop an Uber to the Hyperloop and be there in thirty. Can you pick me up?" I rolled my wheelchair to the kitchen counter and began putting away the salad ingredients I had just gotten out.

"Pick you *up*?" echoed my mother. "Lisa, were you even *listening* to me? Your father has *lost* his mind! He wants me to start packing! I can't leave him *alone*! What if he's *gone* when I get back?"

"I don't think he's going to move immediately, Mom. Not if he wants you to pack for him." As my mother sputtered incoherently, I added, "Never mind. I'll get there. See you in a bit."

I sighed and finished putting my lunch away. I tweeted for an Uber, grabbed my go-everywhere bag, and rolled my chair outside. By the time I got there, the Uber was waiting. The bot helped me get situated and we drove the ten minutes to the Hyperloop. I looked out the window at the rolling sidewalks full of "handicapables" (as my mother insisted on calling us) of all kinds. I marveled again that the Change Council had allowed downtown Seattle to become Club Capable, also known as SeaCap.

True, Seattle had long been one of the most accessible cities, but it was still a surprise when they designated such an important economic trade center as the Club Hub for the disabled. It had been one of the first designations the Council had made, after the agriculture and infrastructure Hubs. I had moved in as soon as I could, but lately I had been having second thoughts. Maybe my Dad had the right idea.

My Dad's greatest passion his whole life, aside from (perhaps) his wife and children, had been golf. He'd been talking about moving to the nearest Club Golf -- I couldn't remember what kitschy name they had selected for it -- for two years. Only someone as practiced at ignoring what she didn't want to know as my Mom would have been taken by surprise at his recent announcement.

When I got to the Hyperloop, I requested, "Bremerton Hyperloop, and an Uber to Kitsap Lake Club." I was told that no such Club existed. The computer and I had a "refreshing little discussion," as my favorite book character, Amelia Peabody, would have expressed it. (Peabody World was my top choice for my next home.) I looked up the gps coordinates and we figured out that Kitsap Lake Club was now Fisherman's Rest.

So, the local Change Council had finally settled on fishing rather than boating for their Club's Subject. Probably that was a good part of the reason my Dad had finally determined to leave. I asked the Hyperloop AI to be sure I got a wheelchair-savvy

Uber for the other side and zipped through to my hometown.

It had been almost ten years since the United Nations had finally been able to get a majority of nations to acknowledge that capitalism and nation states just weren't working for the planet anymore. (China had been the last holdout, and the UN had finally agreed to designate it Club China, so long as they disarmed.) The world had been on the edge of that dystopian future so many sci-fi movies had envisioned, and for awhile it had looked as though it was too late. Billions had died from territorial disputes, epidemics, and food and water shortages -- the tragic irony was that the decrease in population made the Change a little easier.

The model the UN advisers invented was a world of "Clubs," where people would choose to live together based on their personal inclinations, rather than accidents of birth. As with the demise of feudalism, the Change wasn't happening easily or without huge disruptions world-wide. But it was happening. It would have been impossible without the Hyperloops.

Seattle had been a finalist in the Hyperloop One Global Challenge decades ago, and so had been one of the first to get high-speed connections to neighboring cities, even before the Change had been ratified. Now there were Hyperloop tunnels crisscrossing the world.

Bremerton didn't look any different when I exited the Hyperloop at Fourth and Pacific. The fish statue was still catching the fisherman statue as it has for a hundred years. My Uber was waiting and, thanks to programming I had helped write, it knew what to do with my wheelchair.

When the Change had first been announced, living in SeaCap (or Crip City as I liked to call it) had seemed like a great idea. The fact that the Change Council had been willing to create a completely accessible Club-state from my favorite downtown area had seemed like a dream come true. But now that I had been there for a couple of years, the novelty was wearing off. The idea of living with people for a better reason than just a need for accessibility was beginning to be more and more attractive. It might be nice to live with people who shared an actual passion for something, as my Dad wanted to do.

When I got to the house in the little subdivision where I grew up, my Dad was cheerful and oblivious to my mother's panic. That too was normal. "They're calling it the Tee Club," he said happily. "They're using moss instead of grass -- uses less water, you know. I've got a little cottage right on the edge of the 9th hole. Your mother can come visit me whenever she wants and of course I'll come visit her!"

"So, you really are going to move away from her?" I asked, shocked.

He seemed amused. "Is that how she put it? Lisa, you know I've been talking about doing this ever since the Change started." I was following him around the garage as he sorted through his gardening tools. "Now that they've settled on fishing for the subject here, there's just no point in staying."

"They're not going to allow ski-doos?" My Dad adored his ski-doo.

"No; no motors on the lake except fishing boats. All the boaters are leaving." He squeezed past my chair to put a rake, a trowel, and his gardening gloves in a crate.

"Why are you packing those?"

"That's the best part! I get my cottage at the Tee Club for free, because I'm going to help maintain the course. And the agricultural plots. No pesticides, of course, so a lot of manual labor!" He grinned at me. "This is going to be great!" I don't know what my face told him, but he added, "You know I've always wanted to live on a golf course. It used to be too expensive. Anyway, it doesn't make sense for your mother and I to keep rattling around in this house. The only reason we stayed here was because we thought grandkids -- "he wiggled his eyebrows comically, but I didn't feel like laughing -- "would have fun here. But there won't be any fun here now, even when you do have kids. There'll just be *fishermen*." He said it the way a person might say "gasoline" or "cigarette" or some other long-outlawed vice.

"What about Mom's fun?" I demanded.

He stopped and crouched at my side. "Honey, most of your Mom's friends have already left. A lot of them went to that arts and crafts Club they started in eastern Washington. Whether we live here or at the Tee Club, she's still just a Loop away from them."

"Is the cottage accessible?"

"What kind of a question is that? Of course!" He jumped up and began rummaging through his tools again. "Anyway, they're going to perfect those robo-suits any day now and then you'll be walking!"

"I don't think I want to live in a robo-suit," I muttered.

"Oh, pish. Of course, you'll love it. Think how much more independent you'll be!"

"Yeah." I decided I'd had enough of my father's enthusiasm, and I went into the house to deal with my mother's hysterics.

I convinced her to at least go with him and take a look at this cottage. I was sure once she was there, she'd meet some like-minded people, and they would all have a wonderful time griping about their spouses and working on the latest craft craze. I calmed her down enough for her to start making lunch. Thank god. I was starving.

I wheeled over to the sliding glass doors and looked out at her latest craft project, still sitting on the patio. The gay guy from down the street had helped her take the engine out of my Dad's vintage VW and turn the car into a giant flower pot. My Dad had not been pleased when he'd come home from a golfing trip to find his prized Bug looking like something from Munchkin land, with hundreds of flowers spilling out of it. It occurred to me for the first time that maybe he really *didn't* want her to go with him. But surely, he hadn't cared that much about the car. It wasn't as though he needed it. Driving gasoline engine vehicles had been illegal for years, not that you could find the gas anyway. I shook my head and rolled down the hall to my old bedroom.

I'd moved a lot of stuff out, or gotten rid of it, when I'd gone to college, and disposed of a lot more when I'd moved to Club Crip and started working as an Uber programmer. The only things still here were some clothes and personal items for unexpected overnight stays. This wasn't the first time my Mom had been in a panic about something, and I had come rushing home to calm her. I was sure it wouldn't be the last, whether my parents were living together or not. I shivered. I couldn't face the idea of them splitting up.

I chose to think instead about how easy it was to travel now, with Hyperloops everywhere. I had *personally* developed -- and continued to improve -- the crip-friendly Uber AI. I was pretty proud of that.

No, I was really proud of that. Did I want to live in a place where accessibility was not the norm again? It was a hard decision which I wa not going to make right now.

My Dad's ingenuous question, "Is that how she put it?" kept coming back to me. Was it possible my Dad really had gotten fed up with her? Had the Bug been the straw that broke his camel's back? To drag that metaphor a little further, I thought it far more likely my Dad would do the equivalent of a camel's kicking or spitting rather than abandon her. No, he was just pulling her strings again. He'd been doing it all my life, all of their married lives, so far as I could tell. It was just the way they were. Wasn't it?

Mom called me to lunch and I went eagerly, glad to leave my thoughts behind. I had two helpings of the couscous salad, which pleased her. My Dad finished off the homemade garlic bread, clapped his hands and said, "Well, I'm off!"

Mom dropped her fork on to her plate with a clatter.

"Off to...?" I asked.

"To set up my new workroom!"

"We're coming with you," I said firmly. "We want to see this place."

"Oh? Okay, I'll order another Uber."

"Please remember to ask for a crip-savvy one!" I said hastily as he spoke to his phone.

"Lisa!" said my mother sharply.

"Sorry -- handicapable," I amended, sighing. Just about everyone I knew called SeaCap Club Crip, but my Mom still wouldn't let me use the word. She was far more sensitive about my feelings than I was.

Mom was eating her couscous with a determined, martyred air. My Dad got up and took his plate into the kitchen. "Does Carrie know about this decision you've made, Dad?" I asked, looking over the counter at him.

"Your sister has been too busy settling in at Disney World 257 to keep in touch with the likes of us," he said, putting beer in a cooler.

When I saw him adding mustard and catsup, I asked, "Dad, what are you doing?"

"Packing for my lunch tomorrow." Again, my mother's fork clattered to her plate. She got up and left the room. "Pack me some clothes for tomorrow, will you?" he called after her. He picked up the cooler.

I rolled my chair back and blocked him from leaving the kitchen. "Dad, what are you doing?"

"Taking my food out to the Uber."

"You know what I mean." I took a deep breath. "Mom thinks you're deliberately leaving her. Are you?"

He tried to squeeze past me, but he couldn't without hitting me in the head with the cooler. He slammed the cooler onto the kitchen table and gestured toward the patio. "Did you see that?" I didn't bother to answer. I had been here when he'd gotten home and first seen it himself. "Since I retired," he said tightly, "I have golfed, gone out on the ski doo and taken care of that car. Two of those things are done for me here. I am going to go where I can do the third. Your mother is welcome to come if she wants to." He picked up the cooler.

I didn't move. "She doesn't feel welcome. She thinks you don't want her."

He lowered his head and muttered something.

"What?"

"Does she want me?"

"What's that supposed to mean? Of course, she wants you!"

"Yeah? She chose to stay here when I went on that golfing trip. For a week. She chose to turn my classic Bug into a flower garden!"

"Oh, but Dad, you know she doesn't understand --"

"She spent the whole week destroying my car with that young guy from down the street. Most of her friends have already left! If she chooses to stay here now, I have to assume it's because there is some other reason to stay."

I blinked, astonished, and didn't resist when he pushed my chair back and walked past me, holding the cooler high. *He's jealous. My father is jealous of the gay guy from down the street.* I giggled, even as I felt tears come to my eyes. I followed him outside. "Cancel the Ubers, Dad."

"Why? *I*'m still leaving."

"Wait one hour. Please? For me?"

He grumbled about there being no point, but he did it and went back into his garage.

Half an hour later I ushered Rafi and Ethan into the garage and introduced them to Dad. As they shook hands, Rafi said, "I don't think I've met you before, Mr. Harriman. Ethan has worked with your wife on a number of projects, but I'm often out of town."

My father made fake-polite noises to Rafi while glaring at Ethan.

"Oh my god!" said Ethan "I'm so sorry about the car, Mr. Harriman! Your daughter told me you weren't pleased. I had no idea! I assumed your wife, well --" He stuttered to an uncomfortable halt.

Rafi pitched in, "I was out of town that week, or I would have put a stop to their project. Ethan is hopeless when it comes to cars; he doesn't know a thing about what's valuable. I had a classic Hyundai hybrid when we got married and can you believe he wanted me to convert it?"

My father's face was a joy to my eyes. "Married?"

Rafi said, "We've been married for ten years, and this is our first home together. We'll be moving now. We voted for boating."

To give my father some time, I said, "I hear most of Lake Chelan will be a boating Club. You have to be willing to work in the fruit orchards, though."

"Growing fruit?" said Ethan. "I could do that."

"You *are* good at making things grow," said Rafi, grinning at him.

Ethan's face turned red. So did mine. My father said, "I'll say! Those flowers in my classic car are growing like crazy!"

I whispered to Rafi, "You have heard of the so-called Homo-Erectus Club, haven't you?"

His dark brown eyes sparkled. "It's on our list of possibles."

After they left, I went to talk to my red-eyed mother, theatrically draped sideways across their bed. "Dad didn't know Ethan is gay," I said.

She lifted her head and gazed tragically at me. "Your father is oblivious to *so many* things."

I smiled. "He thought you were having an affair with him."

She sat up, tragic heroine forgotten. "He *did?* No! He *couldn't!* Ethan is only about -- what -- thirty-five?"

She stood up and looked at herself in the mirror on the closet door. "Your father thought Ethan would be interested in *me*? That handsome *young* man?" She began rummaging through her closet. "I should put on something more *attractive* if we're going to go see our new home and meet our new neighbors."

As I went back out to the garage, I called for an Uber. "I thought you were going to go with us," said my Dad, overhearing me. "Don't you want to see the place?"

"Not tonight," I said. "Maybe this weekend."

When the Uber pulled up, I realised I had forgotten to ask for a crip-savvy one. "Damnit." I was so used to living in Club Crip where they were all savvy -- thanks to me! -- that I forgot. If I moved to Peabody World, which was part of old Egypt, I would have to change my habits. I scowled to myself. The whole world should be accessible! I had considered joining WWAM (Whole World Accessibility Movement) since it had started. Maybe now was the time. If I could play the diplomat between my parents, I could certainly advocate for the disabled. It would be an interesting new challenge.

My Dad helped the clueless bot to stow my chair. He patted the Uber on its curved hood and said, "You ever noticed how much these things look like Bugs?"

"Yes, Dad. You've mentioned it once or twice before."

My Mom came out in a V-necked dress and sandals. My Dad whistled. "Lookee dat beeyootiful sight!"

"Bye, Mom," I said. "Bye, Dad."

Mom waggled her fingers at me. Dad didn't even hear me.

*

United Nations Resolution - Time for a Change

Purpose: To re-inhabit the earth through a peacefully sustainable model.

Whereas the earth has reached a crisis point which could lead to the extinction of life as we know it; and

Whereas climate change has caused disruptions to global ecosystems such that traditional economies have been disrupted if not destroyed worldwide; and

Whereas migrating/ refugee peoples have created humanitarian crises in nearly every viable country on earth; and

Whereas pandemics have decreased the world's population and left some areas completely uninhabited and others struggling to maintain basic services; and

Whereas historical organizations/ governments have proven incapable of maintaining order under these circumstances; and

Whereas the development of a transportation system through Hyperloops for the world has been shown to be economically feasible;

Now therefore be it here enacted by this United Nations, that a new body shall be created to determine a new world order based on the current capability of the earth's biology and the predicted ongoing effects of climate change on that biology, and on the interests of the people who inhabit it.

- These interests (subjects) will be determined by a worldwide survey to be undertaken by the United Nations immediately.

- The current and future status of the earth's biology will be determined and mapped by an international panel of scientists, beginning immediately.

- A world-wide, free transportation system will be developed with construction of Hyperloops throughout the world.

hen the survey and the map are completed, regions of the world will be assigned to interest groups to suit the needs and abilities of, first, the world as a whole, and, second, the interest groups themselves. Thus, the needs of farming, medical, and energy-producing groups will take precedence over sports, literature, and entertainment groups. No subject area will be large enough to support an army. No alliances will be allowed except to serve food and energy needs.

Ultimately, the world will consist of Club-states, rather than nation-states or city-states. Supplies will be stockpiled for each new Club-state to use until their own economies are organized and operational. UN advisors will be assisting states to become independent as quickly as possible. The land which remains capable of producing food will be used to supply the world. Refugees currently living in unsanitary, disease-ridden camps which are a health danger to us all have priority in finding homes based on their subject-interests. Countries currently at war will be broken up and their people dispersed. An algorithm will be determined for balancing supply, demand, need, population, transportation and packaging requirements for all products and all peoples.

The earth can no longer tolerate the nationalism of past centuries. A new world order must be established or we will all perish.

Resolved this United Nations Day, October 24, 2049

About the Author

Susan McDonough-Wachtman

Susan McDonough-Wachtman has been a burger tosser, customer service rep, curriculum developer, parent, kayaker, gardener, and high school teacher. She's written children's stories, short stories, romances, essays, science fiction, numerous letters to the editor, and a blog. Most recently, "Mother, May I" was accepted for the Halloween edition of Tales From the Moonlit Path, and "Xanthippe" was included in the Brigid's Gate anthology Musings of the Muses. She lives on the coast in the Pacific Northwest with one cat and one husband. *Ferry Findings*, a collection of short stories, is available from Kitsap Publishing, and the science fiction novella, *Snail's Pace*, is now available from Water Dragon Publishing. Find more at *https://susanmcdonoughwachtman.wordpress.com*

www.ingramcontent.com/pod-product-compliance
Lightning Source LLC
LaVergne TN
LVHW041644070526
838199LV00053B/3554